My Friend Is Sad

To my friend Marcia

ISBN-13: 978-0-545-07147-5
ISBN-10: 0-545-07147-X

Text and illustrations copyright © 2007 by Mo Willems.
All rights reserved. Published by Scholastic Inc., 557 Broadway, New York, NY 10012,
by arrangement with Hyperion Books for Children, an imprint of Disney Children's Book Group, LLC.
SCHOLASTIC and associated logos are trademarks and/or registered trademarks of Scholastic Inc.

12 11 10 9 8 7 6 5 4 3 2 1   8 9 10 11 12 13/0

Printed in the U.S.A.   23

First Scholastic printing, January 2008

My Friend Is Sad

By Mo Willems

An ELEPHANT & PIGGIE Book

SCHOLASTIC INC.
New York Toronto London Auckland Sydney
Mexico City New Delhi Hong Kong Buenos Aires

Ohhh . . .

My friend is sad.

Clowns are funny.
But he is still sad.

How can anyone be
sad around a robot!?

Ohhh . . .

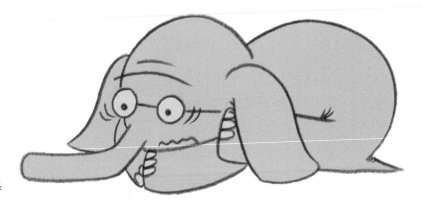

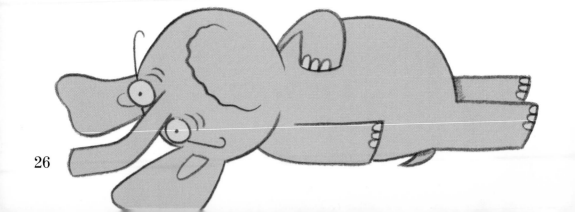

I am sorry. I wanted to make you happy. But you are still sad.

29

You are happy?

But I was so sad, Piggie.
So very SAD!

Then I saw a clown!

40

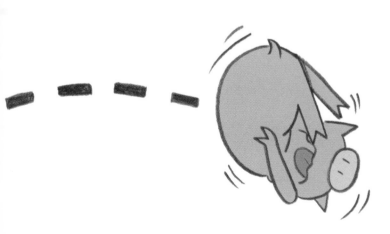

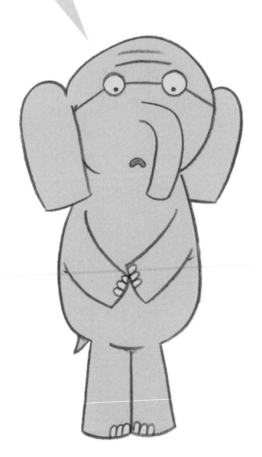

And my best friend
was not there
to see it with me.

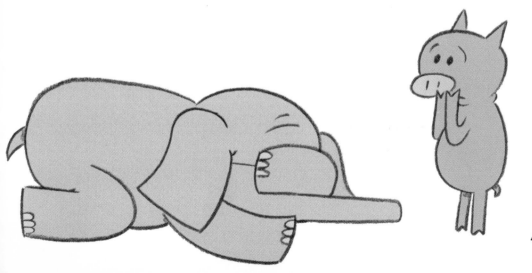

49

My friend is here now!